BOO!

Words and Pictures by

Colin McNaughton

Ⓐ
Andersen Press
London

Through the dark, dark streets of the dark, dark town, Preston (the Masked Avenger) sneaks…

"Boo!" says Preston the Masked Avenger and he disappears into the night.

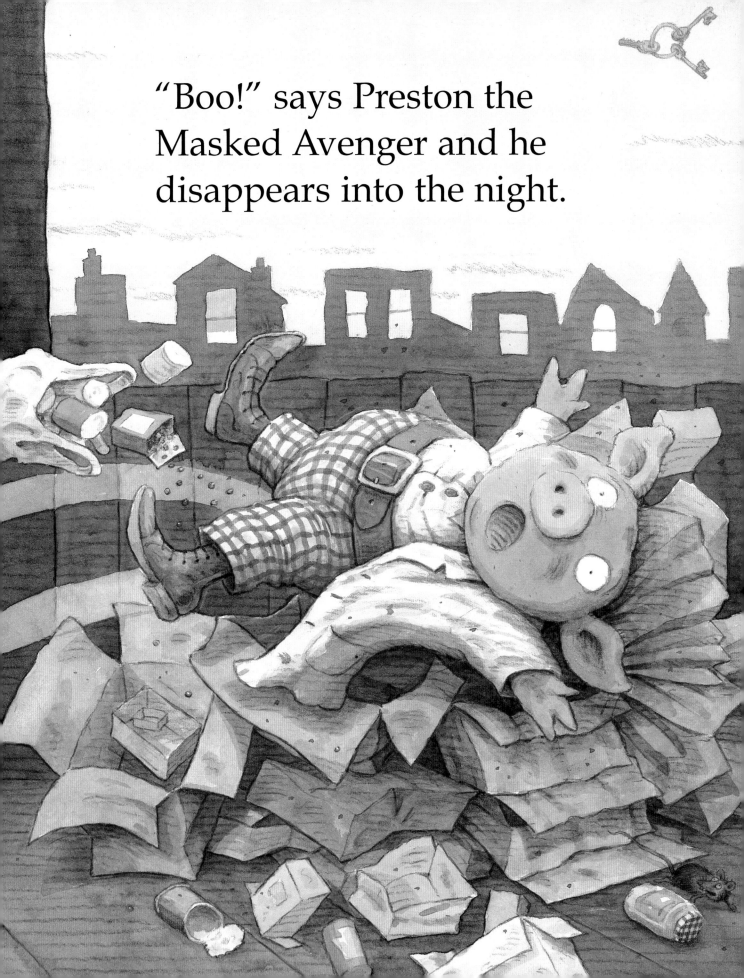

Slinking through the shadows,
Preston the Masked Avenger
spies Billy the Bully,
his next victim...

"Boo!" says Preston the Masked Avenger and he disappears into the night.

Cat-like, Preston the Masked Avenger slides through the darkness until he reaches the school-house where his teacher is working late...

"Boo!" says Preston the Masked Avenger and he disappears into the night.

Next, the super-hero
comes to Mr Wolf's house.
"Boo!" says Preston the Masked
Avenger very quietly and
he sneaks right past.
"I may be a super-hero," says
Preston, "but I'm not daft!"
And he disappears
into the night.

MR.WOLF

NO
WOOD
CUTTERS

Preston the Masked Avenger
lies in wait for the greatest
villain in the universe - his dad.

"Boo!" says Preston the Masked Avenger and he disappears into the night.

(At least, he would have
done if his dad hadn't
grabbed him first.)

"Preston!" says Preston's dad.
"I've had complaints about you
from all over town. You're
a naughty little pig."

Preston the Unmasked
Avenger is sent to his room
without any supper.

Suddenly!

"Boo!" says Preston's dad.
"That'll teach you to go
around scaring people."

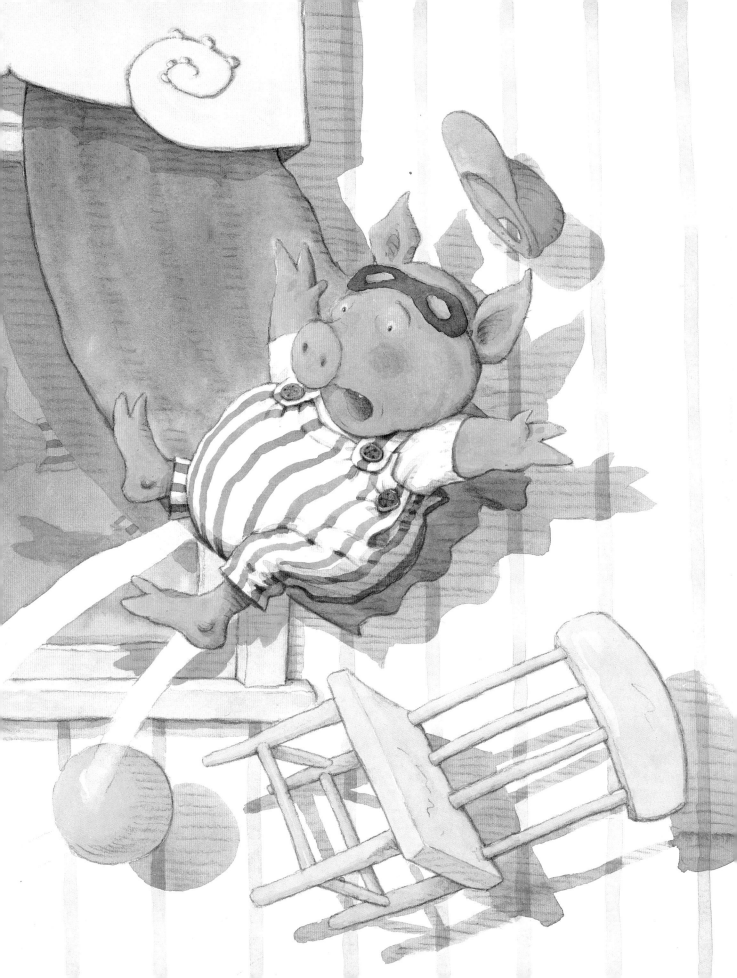

But it doesn't.